The Rou~~n~~

We've all received that a
with the Christmas card, with all the previous
12 months' worth of family news.

Often comprising many pages, and occasionally accompanied by an assortment of photos taken at various family gatherings throughout the year, it has become a bone of contention with many. Do we like them, do we not?

Having been inundated with these missives for many years, and never having written one myself, I thought it may be fun to sit down and rattle off a few. Not to send, but as the subject of a one-off little book which may just resonate with some. Just a touch exaggerated? Maybe, but then again, maybe not! I discovered in the process that there is more than one way to write a Round Robin letter.

If you are a writer of a 'one size fits all', you may just identify with one of these...

Which style is yours??

The Dramatic

Darlings!

Just a 'quickie' to enclose with our Christmas card to all our nearest and dearest!

Well – what a wicked, exciting year it's been for us. Hope it has for all of you too!!

Where to start…??!!

Rupert developed a deathly virus at the beginning of the year. Yikes – it was Scary!! He was on all sorts of medications – nothing diagnosed, so luck of the draw as to what worked. Eventually, after heaven knows how many weeks off work, he was well again and soon back to his chipper self. His resilience knows no bounds!!

Me? I had a Wonderful Surprise in April when Daddy treated me to an early birthday present – a cruise in The Bahamas, no less!! I was allowed to take

Rupert, of course(!) who definitely needed the R&R. We had a Maaarrrrrvellous time and so lovely to be on our own after the traumas of last year; refer to last Round Robin everyone!!!

Cecilia has found The Most Gorgeous Boyfriend – if only I was younger!! He's an architect – not your typical, if there is such a thing. He plays in the wildest rock band every Saturday night called 'The Designers'. We were treated to one of his gigs mid-year – were issued with ear plugs at the door which did little to alleviate the assault to the eardrums, I have to say. SO good though! Hoping to get a recording contract one day.

Humphrey graduates this year. He has had a terrific time at uni studying and playing hard. Not necessarily in that order!! I wonder how he coped with the pressure, but he did. Oh, to be young again and to be able to burn the candle at both ends. Can't you tell I'm feeling my age at last?! I turned 50 in June – yes, really!! Came as a shock which Rupe didn't cushion, by referring to me as his 'little geriatric'! Not amused – and not so little anymore either! I've put on a kilo in the last 6 months despite having joined a local gym where I spend hours pumping iron and treading millions of miles each week. A friend told me it's all muscle so perhaps I should concentrate on body building…?! Have you seen those women? Freaky or what?!!

Annabel is sweet sixteen this year – going on thirty! She's such a little old woman, very organised and knows exactly where she's going. Actually, to Africa at the end of the year where she plans to spend Christmas building wells, or something like that; she wants to do charity work when she leaves school so this is somewhat of a precursor to that.

Still have plans to move house next year. This old rambling mansion is getting too big for us now that C and H have moved out and the grounds are just too much for me, even with the help of our Wonderful Gardener, otherwise known as The Old

Retainer! Rupert wants to move to the coast so he can have the boat for which he has yearned for years, but I still want my little cottage in the Cotswolds. Who doesn't? Will keep you all posted on our movements, IF and WHEN!!

Will 'treat' you all to another update this time next year. How lovely it is to keep in touch this way now that no-one has time for anything more. E-mailing has never been my forte, texting seems so impersonal and pen and ink seem to belong to the age of the dinosaur.

All welcome to drop in anytime – preferably before we move, whilst we have the room!

Wishing you all a Joyous Christmas.

Oodles of love, hugs and kisses. Mwah!!

Caroline   *xxxxxxxxxx*

MAN TO MAN

Felicity has persuaded me — rather forcibly I might add — to write the Xmas letter this year. Frankly, I have no idea where to start. Who invented these things anyway? As you all know, I am not really a good correspondent — in fact the last letter I wrote was to my prospective father-in-law asking for Felicity's hand in holy matrimony, and that's a good few years ago now.

Well, the main news from this end is that the local pub, 'The Cock and Bull' have gone bust. Seems one of the cellar-men was ripping off the odd barrel — and then the landlord's wife did a bunk with one of the barmen. Caused quite a scandal in the village, particularly as the barman was the local vicar's lad, 12 years her junior. Anyway, nowhere local to drink anymore, so will have to get the car out to drive to the next village whenever we want a bevvy or two. Will no doubt result in curbing the intake.

Had to give up playing for the local cricket team this year — age seems to be against me all of a sudden and I can't keep up with the young studs anymore. My bowling average was pretty good but as 12th man I rarely made it to the wicket.

Doctor tells me I have to take it easy too because of high blood pressure, and that I have to lose a few stone — ten was the number mentioned. Maybe the pub going bust was a good thing as I'm pretty sure my well-maintained gut was more than half due to the several pints of bitter I put away every Saturday night. So the wife tells me anyway. That and the ton of chips she serves up nearly every tea time. Have told her to cut down, but will she listen.

Felicity has told me to wind this up sharpish as I've been poring over it for several hours, and she wants me to go and wash the car, pronto. Never a dull moment in this household!

Cheers for now. Have one for me.

Merry Chrimbo to one and all,

Cyril

SMUG NAME DROPPERS

Dear All

Hope this finds everyone well and in the Christmas spirit.

Our year has been exhausting work-wise and also busy with the building of our new house in Dorset. It's been an exciting time after selling our town house for well over the market value, and therefore making a tidy profit. Hence the means, at last to have our luxury house in the country. With six bedrooms and four bathrooms I will have to employ a maid – and a gardener for the four acres! Our new neighbour in Dorset will be Sir Charles Little, the famous landscaper, so we are hoping for some advice from him.

We already have plans for stables and a large lake. Neil, as you know, is a keen fisherman, so wants to fill it with trout and bream, etc.

Both children, Nicholas and Charlotte, have left university with Honours and are already forging careers in banking and with the Foreign Office respectively. We are so proud of them.

Our friend, the Conservative MP for Compton-Banbury, has offered us his lakeside apartment in Tuscany for the summer and, when we return, our house should be finished and ready to move into. You are all welcome to come and stay – preferably not at the same time – although with all the space that probably won't be a problem!

We were lucky to be invited to the premier of the latest James Bond film recently. A dear friend, one of the producers, was able to procure two tickets for us. What a wonderful evening walking the red carpet with all the stars. Lovely to see Dame Judy again.

Neil has been lucky enough to rub shoulders with several well-known athletes through his company becoming involved with the Olympics. One of them, Clive Banks, the rower, has invited him to watch him train on the Thames and afterwards to go for a drink together. What it is to have famous contacts!

Hope next year will be as great for all of you as this year has been for us.

Love and hugs

Pandora

CYNICAL

Well, here we are again, another 'successful' year for all.

Steve out of prison on parole – great to have him home, except he's a bit glum. Mixing with all those psychopaths and axe murderers has given him a wry sense of humour. As he says, what's a bit of fraud between friends? Anyway, he's taken up stamp collecting; not the most exciting of hobbies, but it keeps him out of mischief and when he's shut up in the attic sorting through the Penny Blacks, I can pretend he's still in prison.

My hernia has been playing up – not that bad, but it sometimes feels like my stomach is up in my throat. Can't complain, it could be gall stones or varicose veins, both of which run in the family…

Grandma Jones is showing signs of dementia – got on a bus in Chelmsford and asked for a ticket to Glasgow. It was only going as far as Swindon so I think the driver was a bit confused, not to mention Granny. Hope to have her come and live with us eventually if we can get a self-contained extension built in time before she karks it!

Boys are fine. David is still finding it hard to get a girlfriend and Steve thinks he may be gay. I've told him that wearing a necklace and hair gel is not a sign that he's that way inclined, they all do it these days, don't they, but I did catch him the other day trying on one of my dresses, so not sure what that means.

Gary has become a little deaf of late – although a friend did point out the other day that 14 year-olds do suddenly develop a selective sense of hearing. Anyway, asking him to take out the rubbish or clean his school shoes gets little response. Have booked him in for a hearing test early next year.

I keep busy with my library duties twice a week and recently became a 'lollipop lady'. Had a close call the other day when a child ran out into the road in front of an oncoming lorry. Luckily missed her by the skin of her left leg, but I'm now waiting for a letter from the Council asking for my resignation. I mean, not my fault, but they have to find a scapegoat I suppose.

Only joking about all of the above, but so little has happened this year and I really didn't want to bore you with our very ordinary lives. I had to write something though – hope it gives you all a smile!!

Happy Christmas to all. Look forward to hearing all your (much more exciting) news.

Much love from all of us,

Sue

OUT OF THE BLUE

Christmas has come around again and what better time to reflect on life and to get in touch with long lost friends.

I know it is a very long time since many of you have heard from me, and for that I apologise. I left England some years ago after a traumatic time in my life, and did so without leaving any forwarding address. The time now seems right for me to attempt to explain a little of what happened, why I left so suddenly, and to try and reconnect with you all.

Most of you knew Richard, my husband, but perhaps not what he was like. Over the three years of our marriage he became an addicted gambler and in the process we lost just about everything. He lost his job and our house was eventually re-possessed. I also discovered that he had been having an affair for several months. I was at the time at a very low ebb, emotionally.

My salvation came, in effect, when an old school friend, Fiona, invited me to stay with her and her husband Angelo in Malta. I packed an overnight bag and literally left on the next plane. My parents had both died within months of each other the year before so I felt there was nothing left for me in England. I cut all ties with my former life – good friends included, sadly. I had found it difficult to confide in anyone and no-one, as far as I know, knew about Richard's gambling or affair/s... I guess there had been more than one.

I ended up staying in Malta, went back to nursing, found a little flat in Sliema and eventually met a lovely man, Marco, a doctor at the hospital where I worked. We were married 6 years ago and have 2 lovely children, Stefan and Helena. I have never been happier. Life is good at last.

I would love it if you feel able to get in touch after all this time and to tell me all about your lives and what you have been up to over the last ten years. We are coming to England this summer and it would be lovely to get together with as many of you as possible, and to perhaps renew old friendships.

With all my love

Monica

DOOM AND GLOOM

Dear Friends

What a year we've had. So much to tell and so little time. Poor Marty was diagnosed with kidney stones earlier in the year and had to undergo a very painful operation. He was in hospital for ten days and when he came home sunk into a deep depression. It has been trying for all of us, not least the children who have been treading on eggshells around him. The firm are holding his job open for him but no-one is sure when he will be able to return.

I've been working in the local bakery every hour known to man for the last six months which, juggling that with running the house single-handedly, not to mention looking after 5 children is wearying in the extreme. The eldest two took their respective 'O' and 'A' levels this year and have done okay. At least they have the necessary results to follow their chosen professions. Christian got 3 'A' levels and is hoping to join a local paper as a junior reporter, but so far there has been nothing available locally. He may have to venture further afield, although he is loath to leave home at present. Jonathan has left school with 8 'O' levels and wants to be a plumber; he didn't need the 'O' levels but they may be useful if he changes his mind down the track. There are few apprenticeships available at the moment, unfortunately, so he may have to think of something else to do in the meantime.

Could really do with a holiday but no expectations of one in the near future. We had booked a week in Blackpool in September but had to cancel when Marty was no better.

My sister is getting married for the third time, in February. A low-key affair this time and we have offered to have a small reception here for them – although if Marty isn't better by then we may have to reconsider. Nothing extravagant anyway, just a small party for half a dozen family and close friends. I have offered to make the cake and will get a friend to ice it. Not much good at the fancy stuff.

Mum and Dad moved into a Retirement Home in August, just up the road. They were both sad to give up their own home but were finding it hard to cope. We are a bit disappointed in the standard of care, not enough staff I think. There have been some grim reports about Care Homes in the news recently so we are keeping a careful eye out. I have complained about some of the practices and am waiting for a response.

We had to have our old Tilly put down last month, at last. She was 17 and could hardly get around in the end. It was very sad to see her go having had her since a small puppy. I don't think we shall have another dog, they are so tying.

Well, I do hope this hasn't sounded too depressing. I've just read over it and it sounds as if we're having a dull old life, but I can't find much positivity at the moment. However, we are looking forward to Christmas spent at home. Hope to have Mum and Dad out for the day if they're up to it. Hopefully Marty will rouse himself and the New Year will bring us better luck. Hope the same for all of you.

Best regards to all
Kerry

A BOGAN ONE...
(Warning – coarse language)

G'day folks,

Just come in from lighting the barbie – Sheila wants to throw a few prawns on for lunch, so while she's doing that, I thought I'd scribble a few lines to all you bastards, far and wide.

Just gotta say to all my Pommie friends – what about the cricket. Aussies slaughtered the lotta you good an' proper in the last one-day series... 'bout bloody time. Bring on the Ashes – hope we can do some more damage on home soil.

Kids are alright. Shane made captain of the team, so I've become a reluctant AFL fan since we've been down in Melbourne. It's all great footy to me whatever the code, as long as I've got a coldie in my hand and my feet up.

Kylie's gonna teach at a school in The Alice come the start of next year. She spent most of her gap year in pommie-land, living and working in Earls Court, aka Kangaroo Valley. Looked up a few rellies whilst she was over there - my lot are originally from Belfast, so gave her an excuse to see something of The Emerald Isle and to learn about her heritage. We're all into that over here, finding our roots and all, convict or free settler, whatever.

Sheila and I are taking off up to Cairns for the summer, we'll need a cut lunch and a water bag to get there. Desperate for some sun. I've had a gut-full of Melbourne's 'Four Seasons in One Day' crap, I'm a bloody Queenslander.

Have just bought myself a van, (a Winnebago as Sheila calls it) so we're ready to hit the road when we eventually retire and join the Grey Nomads, which is the thing to do round here, apparently. There's a lot of country out there. Lived here all my life, but still haven't made it as far as Perth, Darwin or even the GAFA (aka the Great Australian F... All). I'd be happy to take off with just my swag and billy, but the missus needs somewhere to plug in her bloody hair dryer.

Meanwhile, I've been talked into joining a ballroom-dancing class (yeah, no shit). The old girl was hooked on 'Dancing with the Stars', so now we're learning how to frolic around like bloody galahs. I was as nervous as a turkey on

Christmas Eve at first, but now I'm getting the hang of it. Hugh Jackman eat your heart out.

Hope to see some of you down-under next year – always up for a stubby, so let us know if you're over this way. Trying to do our bit for Aussie tourism in the wake of the downturn due to floods, fires, cyclones, shark attacks etc. So, in the infamous words of the legendary Lara Bingle – 'Where the Bloody Hell Are Ya?'

Have y'selves a fair dinkum Xmas, wherever you are. We'll be on a beach somewhere, me in my green and gold budgie smugglers, but will spare a thought for those of you shivering your arses off elsewhere.

Bruce and Sheila.

THE TICK AND FLICK

For those who want to include all the family news in their Christmas cards, but don't have time even to write the traditional Round Robin, here's a fast, easy way to get the same result – it's called 'The Tick and Flick'. (Thought up by a man – of course!).

Tick where appropriate:

☐ Promoted
☐ Demoted
☐ Changed jobs
☐ Retired

☐ Moved house
☐ Upgraded
☐ Down-sized
☐ Renting
☐ Squatting
☐ Gone into a home

HOLIDAYS THIS YEAR:

☐ Britain
☐ Europe
☐ Asia
☐ USA
☐ Africa
☐ Australia
☐ The Moon
☐ Elsewhere
☐ Nowhere

CHILDREN'S ACHIEVEMENTS

- ☐ Accepted for Oxbridge
- ☐ A grades in all subjects
- ☐ Respectable passes in most subjects
- ☐ Failed miserably in all subjects
- ☐ Dropped out of school and now living with a dodgy friend in a Council flat in Fulham

PETS

- ☐ Bought a pedigree Rottweiler puppy
- ☐ Adopted dog and 2 cats from the RSPCA
- ☐ Budgie died so up-scaled to a parrot which can already say 'you are the weakest link'
- ☐ Training a Guide Dog called Gordon
- ☐ Don't like pets

OTHER EXCITING EVENTS

- ☐ Big 60th birthday bash
- ☐ Big retirement party
- ☐ Huge 30th celebrations
- ☐ Got married for the first time
- ☐ Got married for the second time
- ☐ Daughter gave birth to twins/triplets
- ☐ Son passed driving test
- ☐ Son failed driving test
- ☐ Others
- ☐ None

SPORTY STUFF

- ☐ Family member selected for Olympic Games
- ☐ "   "   "   "   "   "   County
- ☐ Joined local tennis club
- ☐ Joined local sports club (social events only)
- ☐ Joined gym
- ☐ Cancelled gym membership
- ☐ Won 3-legged race at local fete

(Insert signature here)

………………………………………………..

ALL SENTENCES STARTING WITH 'I' OR 'WE' AND OTHER PERSONAL PRONOUNS

(By definition, most Round Robins favour the 'I' and 'we' pronoun – but some are more exaggerated than others, as the one below illustrates).

We have had a fairly ordinary year – not that much to tell, but nonetheless, will get you up to date.

I had a 'big op' at the beginning of the year. I'd been having problems for a while so in the end had to go under the knife. I won't go into the gory details, but suffice to say I'm feeling so much better and ready for anything, once more!

We had a wonderful family holiday in Scotland with all the children and their partners over Easter. Our accommodation was splendid, right on the edge of Loch Lomond and weather as perfect as could be for that part of the world. I, nor any of the others, sighted Nessie, but we had fun looking!!

I organised a surprise party for Seamus's 60th in September – he swore he didn't guess, but did question the amount of food piling up in the fridge at one point! I made his favourite Coronation Chicken and lots of different salads, plus loads of puds. We all had a fantastic time and took at least a week to recover. We were all ready for another holiday then!

Our honeymoon (all those years ago!), we spent in Majorca, so we decided to return to Spain – this time touring the northern part, including the Picos de Europa National Park; we thought the scenery out of this world . I, for one, thought it the best holiday we have had in many years and recommend it thoroughly.

My job has been a bit erratic over the last six months and so I have gone down to three days a week, which is giving me lots of time to do all the things I'd promised myself over the years. I've taken up tai chi and have joined a book club. My reading matter has become more interesting and I'm re-reading a lot of the classics I loved as a girl, plus all the latest best sellers – my favourite at the moment is Anita Shreve's 'Fortune's Rocks'; she also wrote 'The Pilot's Wife' – both well worth a read for all my book loving friends.

Our children have been busy with their respective lives. Naomi has just changed jobs, moved house and – not least – become engaged! We're delighted of course – Simon is absolutely lovely. We had guessed for a while that he was planning to propose, and as it turned out he did so whilst they were holidaying in Barbados. We all thought it very romantic.

We are also very proud of Damien who graduated from medical school with Honours in June. He has worked so hard over the last five years and is now more than ready for the challenge of becoming a junior houseman at Bristol General.

I am meeting up with my pen-pal from Canada in June – the first time we will have met after forty years of correspondence. I have booked us a hotel in London for the first three nights she is here and then she and I plan to drive up to Edinburgh for a 'wee while' – her grandparents were born in Scotland and she wants to try and trace her roots. Seamus and I are then off to Ireland in September to join his parents in celebrating their Golden Wedding anniversary.

We have, as you can see, a couple of things booked and ready for the New Year and I'm sure we will think of more things to do and see as we chug our way through the next twelve months – we always seem to have something happening!

We both send our warm and sincere best wishes to everyone and hope to see as many of you as possible before next Christmas.

Our love to all

Ingrid and Seamus

GERIATRIC NEWS
(donated by mother-in-law!)

Well, Christmas is nearly here again and nothing much happened this year, as usual.

We shall have our customary gathering at my house on Christmas Day. This will include Mrs Murgatroyd from Number 19, Mr Ogilvy in his wheelchair (we somehow manage to get him up the steps and into the house), Mrs Jennings who comes with the help of her Zimmer-frame, and my best friend, Betty, who arrives under her own steam in spite of her arthritis, weak bladder and constipation.

Poor Mrs Murgatroyd, who is 85, had a very nasty accident in April when she was mangling her washing and inadvertently mangled her fingers. Whilst she was in hospital, her son, Jason, sold the mangle and bought a front loader washing machine. When poor Mrs M returned home, she could not understand the instruction book, so now Jason has to come every Thursday after work and do the washing. Serves him right, he shouldn't have interfered.

I have been in and out of the doctor's surgery with various things, but the worst was when I had a fall and broke my hip earlier this year. I was in hospital for some time, thoroughly miserable as they would not let me smoke my cigarettes. As you know, I have been a 20-a-day puffer for years, so it was sheer misery. The food was awful too, so it was very good to get home.

Tragedy struck early in October when Mr Ogilvy fell off his horse while riding. (He had to be winched on board, but once seated was quite able to ride – slowly). He was severely shaken up and the paramedics insisted on taking him to hospital. Poor old boy had broken one or two bones and had to have his legs protected by a cage. Perhaps he should give up riding altogether as he is now in his 90th year.

Horror of horrors! Betty's daughter arrived yesterday unannounced and has whisked her mother off to Northumberland for Christmas and an extended stay. I think I should start looking for an Old Peoples' Home after Christmas where I may rest my weary head and be waited on hand and foot.

I won't bother writing a Round Robin letter next year as I may not have any friends left, so don't look forward to one.

Happy Christmas.

Mabel

PEOPLE WE DON'T KNOW

It doesn't seem a year ago since I last sat down to write to everyone, but here we are again 12 months later and with lots of news to impart.

Our dear friends, Mike and Sally, with whom we went to New York last Christmas, have just moved into a lovely new home near Chester. We went to see them just after their move and spent 2 days happily helping them unpack. They should be straight by Christmas and looking forward to spending it with their children and respective parents.

Mike's cousin, Peter and his wife, Brenda, are in the throes of emigrating to New Zealand and so it has been a sad time for the family saying our goodbyes. We hope to visit them in the not too distant future, once they have settled down. Peter is going to a job with an IT company in Wellington and Brenda is hoping to continue with her nursing in a local hospital. They have found good schools for their children, Wendy and Patrick, both of whom seem very excited about the move.

My sister Patricia and her family have moved again with the Air Force and are now based near Cambridge. Husband Derek has been promoted to Staff Sergeant and will be employed on the helicopters based there. We will be spending Christmas and New Year with them this year which will give us an opportunity to visit other old friends who live just outside Peterborough and my maiden aunt, Auntie Doris, who is in a Home in Ipswich. Auntie Doris is a retired head-mistress whom I sometimes think feels she is still in charge of a classroom of naughty children - and is thus very intimidating! It will be nice to see her though and we will take her a box of her favourite shortbread biscuits and a couple of Agatha Christie thrillers.

Our two have been invited to go on a holiday to Portugal next summer with some old family friends who have a time-share in the Algarve. It really is lovely of them and the girls are very excited. Pam and Roger have two children roughly the same age as our two and have been going to Portugal for many years. I knew Pam when we were single and working together at the local news-agency. Pam is a little older than me and was married quite a bit before me, but we kept up the friendship. She went back to university recently to do a business degree and is thoroughly enjoying being a student at the ripe old age of 40!

My mother's old neighbour, Mr Samuels, died suddenly last month. It was a terrible shock as Mum used to go in to check on him every day. She found him in his favourite armchair where he had evidently quietly passed away. It was quite a drama as the police had to be called and there will now be a post mortem into the cause. He was a lovely old man who had been very kind to our family over the years - a retired bus driver whose wife died some years ago. They had no children, so it's all rather sad.

My God-daughter has just sat her entrance exam to Southampton University. She wants to be a vet like her father. She is a lovely girl whom we all thought would go into modelling as she's 6' tall and very glamourous. We hope to see her and her family early in the New Year when they pass by on their way back from Scotland where they go every year to celebrate Hogmanay. Mum is Scottish and likes to celebrate the New Year in the traditional Scottish manner.

I know I say it every year, but we hope to see more of you all next year. As they say, 'don't be a stranger'! We will certainly endeavour to impose ourselves on as many of you as possible, but with work pressures and other commitments time is limited. Roll on retirement!!

Wishing you all a Merry Christmas and a happy, healthy New Year.

Lots of love from us all

Amanda

EMPTY NESTERS

Life has never been so good, now that we're in our prime,
So much to do, so much to see, with barely ample time.
Each year goes fast, but then it does as we advance in age,
But more and more we find our friends are much on the same page.

We've spent this year in seeing you, as many as we could,
Plus, places new, and older haunts, and those we knew we should.
From York to Rome, and others more far flung,
We've travelled far, walked and explored, and climbed that extra rung!

With children gone and no more pets, our ties are less and less,
We love that we can do 'our thing' in any mode of dress!
Our time's our own and we are free to do just as we please,
To get up late, to go for strolls, forever take our ease.

Christmas then is here again, another year gone by,
Another to look forward to, to gaze up at the sky.
To smell the roses, swim a lap, lie back and just relax
Remembering when we were young, sans stiff and aching backs!

To our friends, this time of year is when we think of you,
Remembering all the years gone past, there's been more than a few!
We wish you well and hope to see you more in years to come,
To raise a glass of wine, a gin; our Navy friends, a rum?!

Until then, we'll just 'enjoy', continue with the flow
We think of you and love you all, in case you didn't know!

The Poets!

FACTUAL AND TO THE POINT

Hi Everyone!

Christmas is nearly here again, so time for the yearly update.

Another successful academic year for the children with twins both getting straight A's in all their A levels. James considering his options. Hoping eventually to get into Leeds to study Biochemistry. Both he and Sarah taking Gap Year and heading Down Under after Christmas.

Sarah still undecided whether to go into Medicine or Law. The world is her oyster and neither of us want her to rush into anything.

Barry got long overdue and much deserved promotion at beginning of year and now heads up large team of accountants at his old firm.

I retired from teaching this year and have taken up volunteer work. Almost busier than before; love being able to 'give back'. Still have a little left-over time to attend to ever demanding garden and to walk dogs.

Speaking of which, Cadbury now almost totally deaf and only responds when I clap my hands loudly. He was 15 this year and arthritis has really got a grip on him. Rowntree just turned 6 - still full of beans although gave us a fright earlier in year when she ingested rat poison and had to have full blood transfusion.

Family holiday this year was Marbella. Excellent accommodation in small hotel just off main street within easy walk of beach. Barry had bad case of food poisoning on second day after eating paella at sea front café, but fully recovered within 48 hours. All came back with respectable sun tans.

Barry and I enjoyed long weekend on Norfolk Broads in April. Showery, but otherwise weather held and we managed to successfully manoeuvre a 40' canal boat through 20 miles of waterway. Lovely scenery.

That concludes our news for this year.

Wishing you all the best for Christmas and New Year.

Love,

Sandra

NOTE BY NUMBERS
(ACTUALLY HAD ONE LIKE THIS ONE YEAR!)

HI ONE AND ALL!

HAVE HAD SIX, MUCH NEEDED 'BREAKS' THIS YEAR — LUCKY US!

1. **JANUARY** — A LONG WEEKEND IN PARIS — JUST THE TWO OF US. DEAD ROMANTIC!

2. **APRIL** — A WEEK IN PEMBROKESHIRE WITH MUM AND DAD — WEATHER VERY WET BUT GREAT TO SHARE SOME TIME WITH THEM, AWAY FROM IT ALL!

3. **MAY** — ANOTHER LONG WEEKEND — JUST NICK AND ME; PRAGUE THIS TIME. A WONDERFUL, BEAUTIFUL CITY AND GREAT FOR A SHOT OF CULTURE.

4. **AUGUST** – A week long cruise on the Danube courtesy of the Company. Nick's prize for being top salesman of the month!

5. **SEPTEMBER** – 5 days in Edinburgh, taking in The Festival. My favourite city!

6. **NOVEMBER** – A long weekend in the Lake District, ostensibly for cousin George's wedding. Great location on the banks of Lake Windemere. A bit damp, but then what do you expect in The Lakes?!

Happy Christmas to everyone

Love

'The Holidaymakers'

IS THIS ONE THE QUEEN WOULD WRITE?

My Dear Subjects

My husband and I - oh dear – did I really ever say that? How Royal of me! We are not amused, as my dear great, great grandmother would have said!

A not quite so 'annus horribilis' this year, although have had to cope with a few unprecedented events within the family. We have become great grandparents yet again. Archie arrived earlier this year. Um - not really a royal name, but we must move with the times. Harry is so hands on, which is very good to see – unlike me with my own children. Give me my time again and I would probably have done things differently - but then things were not the same back then.

We now have 7 or 8 great grandchildren, I think. I really have lost count. Only one more expected from Harry and Megan since they announced that bringing more than two into the world, the way it is – climate change etc. - would be irresponsible. They do seem a very modern couple. I am sad to see them move away but you can't tie the young ones down these days.

Andrew has caused us a few head-aches, but fortunately other events in the world this year have taken the heat off him somewhat.

Philip has had more than his share of illness in recent months but rallies each time, just like the Greek economy. He stays home a lot more but enjoys family gatherings, such as weddings and christenings.

Brexit has been causing us much concern. We tried to stay out of the debacle, which is what it became, we have to privately admit, but we did manage to find ourselves embroiled at one stage, which caused more than a few raised eyebrows amongst those who feel we are above politics. We have always, in the past, maintained a neutral position, but somehow we managed to get forced into a decision to dismiss parliament, which if we had not could have caused a constitutional crisis. Oh dear, and we thought we were doing so well.

We have, this year, had my 94th birthday and have never felt so good. Ever ready for entertaining foreigners and natives alike. It's a big job but we're still up for it. We hope to shake hands with lots more of you next year – and are always happy for a chat – just make it quick; so many of you and so little time.

Please feel free to pop into Buck House or Windsor if you're passing. They tell us that the entrance fees are staying the same for the next 12 months at least, so make it this year if you can before inflation kicks in once more.

Don't forget to watch our speech on Christmas Day – will make it short and snappy for those that can't stand long speeches. Me neither, but we have acquired a knack for coping with them over the years – a quick nap with eyes wide open; takes practice but it is achievable.

Tidings of Joy to all (still my favourite perfume) – hope Phil doesn't forget to get me a bottle this year.

Queen Liz

THROUGH THE EYES OF A CHILD

(Dear All, just haven't had time this year to write my usual epistle, so have handed the task to 12-year-old William – he came first in English this year so I think he is more than qualified!)

Dear Aunties, Uncles and all our friends

Mum has asked me to write this as she doesn't have time – something about cooking, shopping, wrapping presents, hanging decorations, and something else which I didn't get... "stuff the round robin"; (weird 'cos I thought we were having turkey).

By the way, I came second in English, not first, but Mum does like to exagerate. Can't spell that, which is probably why I came second. Dad, being an English teacher was a bit dissapointed (don't think that's the right spelling either) but I did better in maths than last year so that made up for it – I hope!

Have had a wicked year. Went to the best theme park ever in the summer hols. Lots of awesome rides. My best friend Hugh, came with us and Beth took her BFF, Charlotte. The wimpy girls didn't like the Cliff Hanger, but Hugh and I couldn't get enough even if we did have to queue for an hour each time. Hugh spewed all over Mum's skirt after the third ride.

School is ok. I'm doing French this year and hope to go to Brittany in the summer on exchange. Beth went last year and said it was brilliant but her French is still pretty bad, so am not sure it was worth it. That's what Dad says anyway.

Mum changed her job last month. She was working in a Care Home in the next village, but she had a fall out with the matron, or manager, or someone. Said it was a crap job anyway (Mum will probably make me take that out). She now goes 3 days a week to a disabled boy down the road to help him get in and out of bed – and other things. Just lent him my whole set of Harry Potter.

Dad has just applied to be the Principal at school. Don't much fancy being called into the Headmaster's office any more – maybe he'll just wait to beat me with the slipper when I get home. Only joking. He doesn't believe in capital or corporate(?) punishment – and doesn't own a pair of slippers.

Looking forward to Christmas. We have most of the grandparents coming - the three remaining ones that is. Hoping for some good presents. Grandpa Sid is usually the most generous - bought me some cool speakers last year while all I got from Grandma and Grandpa Bennett was a 2 pounds book token for WH Smith. Went a third of the way towards the latest Harry Potter, so shouldn't grumble.

Hope you all get some wicked presents.

Happy Crimble!

Will

SAD AND POETIC

The dappled winter sun is glinting at me through the bare branches of the solitary maple in our little courtyard as I write this in my now, quite bare, attic study.

This room is not what it once was – the shelves shorn of books and files, all now neatly stowed in boxes ready to be moved, nothing on the wall. Our new home is waiting for us, already vacated – a small semi in suburbia surrounded by dense woodland – a leafy wonderland creating an idyllic setting for what should be a long and blissful retirement. We were seduced by the birdsong when we first set eyes on number 33 Acacia Avenue – a sound resonant of the countryside for which we have yearned for so long.

The city lights, the hustle and bustle of a crowded metropolis I shall not miss. Our children say I will, but my days of crowded tubes, long and sometimes demented hours behind a desk, and noisy, bustling wine bars after work are already becoming a fading memory.

We have, for so long, looked forward to long, aimless walks in the countryside. The coast too beckons. The sound of crashing breakers on the stony shores and sandy beaches of Dorset, the Broads perhaps in the summer. We have often dreamt of long summer days spent navigating the beautiful waterways of England and Wales. So much to look forward to – and yet.

I have no idea how long we will be able to enjoy, together, those long-awaited days of retirement. Gloria's Alzheimer's is becoming worse. I fear that, in the not too distant future, it will be necessary for her to be admitted to a private care home. I cannot bear the thought of being without her by my side. We have been together for forty years. 33 Acacia Avenue should be our sanctuary but yet, without her there with me, it may become my hell.

I shall not send this letter after all – I have no wish to burden my dear friends with my sadness. Instead, they will receive a simple card with nothing more than…

HAPPY CHRISTMAS TO YOU, OUR DEAREST FRIENDS

FROM HENRY AND GLORIA

FOR BOOK LOVERS EVERYWHERE!

Hello to all my book-loving friends! Hope you've all managed to catch up on lots of reading this year, or at least made a dent in those 100 books you have to read before you die! In keeping with the 'bookish theme', I thought I would take a novel approach to my Christmas letter this year... enjoy!

GREAT EXPECTATIONS: My niece, Phoebe, gave birth to twins in January, one of each – mother and babies all well. Suggested they be called Pip and Estella, but they are instead to be called Will and Kate!

WUTHERING HEIGHTS: Charles and two friends made it as far as Everest Base Camp in February, a long-held dream of his. May make the summit next time!

LITTLE WOMEN: The girls are growing up fast – Harriet is 14 in March, Sarah 12 in April. Both still loving their ballet and piano.

THE POTATO FACTORY: I took over a small allotment this year and have had limited success with various veg and herbs. I did, though, have some lovely new potatoes and lots of runners – most of which I gave away!

THE INCREDIBLE JOURNEY: I flew out to Australia with my sister in May for a month to see our cousins in Perth whom we hadn't seen for almost 20 years. A long way but had a stopover in Singapore for a few days coming back, which helped break it up.

GONE WITH THE WIND: Charles had a colonoscopy in June. (Sorry, had to include that!).

FAR FROM THE MADDING CROWD: We took a short break, away from it all, in September, on the Isle of Skye. Beautiful, isolated and a chance to re-charge the batteries.

THE GIRL WITH THE DRAGON TATTOO: Clive's new girlfriend, Sue, sports a very striking 'tramp stamp' on her left shoulder. Otherwise a lovely girl!

WATERSHIP DOWN: The girls' have 2 new pet rabbits. To our dismay, having been assured they were both female, babies are expected soon... uggh!

2,000 LEAGUES UNDER THE SEA: Charles is planning on taking scuba diving lessons prior to us going to The Maldives next year. Have to keep reminding him he doesn't like the water since he nearly drowned in Morecambe Bay 2 years ago!

HOW GREEN WAS MY VALLEY: The grass is finally recovering after Charles spilled a whole bottle of weed killer in the middle of the lawn in April!

And finally: *A CHRISTMAS CAROL:* Wishing all our family and friends a merry Christmas. Here's to a new chapter!

With loving wishes,

Jane and Charles xx

A FAIRY STORY!

Once upon a time, there was a girl called Rose and a boy called Toby. They lived in a village surrounded by beautiful woodland. There was a duck pond, a little school, a row of thatched cottages, a grocery shop and an old-fashioned sweet shop which sold barley sugar sticks, humbugs and gob-stoppers.   Toby was particularly partial to the humbugs.

One day, they decided to take a drive out of their village to another village, far away. It was very similar to the village they lived in, except it was bigger, had more shops, two schools and a train station. It was also nearer to Toby's work in the big smoke.

Rose and Toby had two beautiful children called Benjamin and Belinda. Benjamin played the violin and hoped to go to university in the big city when he left school, to study music. Belinda loved horse riding and ballet.

On this day in mid-summer when the sun was high in the sky and making everything look beautiful they found, in this new village, a perfect house with a large, magical garden full of sweet-smelling roses and flower beds connected by little winding paths, a fish pond and other delightful surprises. All four fell in love with it, so much so that they decided to buy it.

Just a few months later they moved to their new house, which they called Paradise. The name of the house was actually 'Longbourne', but they secretly called it Paradise, because that was what it felt like.

Benjamin and Belinda started at their new school and soon made lots of new friends. Benjamin joined the orchestra and the choir and Belinda soon made the netball team and became a member of the debating society.

Rose revelled in her new environment and was soon involved in lots of new activities – church flowers, village fete committee and a power-walking group which met at 7am every Saturday, come blustery wind, glaring shine, freezing hail or squally rain.

Their happiness knew no bounds. Toby had to find a new source for his humbugs, but soon discovered other joys, like the local watering hole which served real ale and other boutique beers.

They hope to live happily ever after in their new fairy-land: address: Longbourne, 3 Ivy Lane, Little Hampstead, Kent.

Wishing all our readers an unreal Christmas!!

ONE FOR 2020

To One and All,

This comes at the end of a year which has seen us all go through the most difficult of times. Some of you have had to cope with the worst kind of sadness, losing loved ones, and I cannot begin to imagine how that has been.

A terrible year too for those who suddenly found themselves without a job and with no certainty as to whether those jobs will still be available when things return to normal. Whatever 'normal' now means.

For others more fortunate, all we seem to have lost is our freedom to socialise, to obtain some of the so-called 'basics' and to holiday abroad. The uncertainty of how long it is all going to last, and most important of all, how long before a vaccine is found, have become the over-riding questions.

For those of us who are retired, life probably didn't feel too different at first. Getting up in the morning knowing that the usual daily tasks awaited us. Then as the reality of the situation kicked in, starting to look for and subsequently find those jobs that we had put off for months – years even! Touching up much needed outdoor paintwork, cleaning out cupboards that we hadn't delved into for months, sorting through boxes of old photographs, looking through recipe books to get new inspiration, etc., became the norm. And, not least, digging over neglected garden beds, prompting us to put in a variety of 'exotic' vegetables in order to become more self-sufficient. Even some of us setting up a hydroponic system! And taking solitary walks became a regular thing.

Hardest thing for many of us has been not being able to see and get together with our families; elderly parents, children and grandchildren. I think that that, on its own, brought home to us how serious this whole situation has been. Self-isolation, personal protective equipment, social distancing, flattening the curve and lock-down, are expressions which we were not familiar with before, but which now are words we will always associate with this period in our history.

When this is all over, I hope that we are all able to become more resourceful, generally happier with our lot and able to find more enjoyment in the simple things of life, in the knowledge that we have survived the worst pandemic in a hundred years. And most importantly, to be more caring and thoughtful of others.

Wishing us all a peaceful and safe Christmas.

Printed in Great Britain
by Amazon